HIC

HIC

MONSTER'S BIRTHDAY HICCUPS

Virginia Mueller
pictures by Lynn Munsinger

Albert Whitman & Company, Morton Grove, Illinois

Other Books about Monster

A Halloween Mask for Monster
Monster and the Baby
Monster Can't Sleep
Monster Goes to School
A Playhouse for Monster

Library of Congress Cataloging-in-Publication Data

Mueller, Virginia.
    Monster's birthday hiccups / Virginia Mueller :
pictures by Lynn Munsinger.
    p. cm.
    Summary: At his birthday party, nothing helps
Monster get rid of his hiccups until he has a
wonderful idea.
    ISBN 0-8075-5267-4 (lib. bdg.)
    [1. Hiccups—Fiction. 2. Birthdays—Fiction.
3. Parties—Fiction. 4. Monsters—Fiction.]
I. Munsinger, Lynn, ill. II. Title.
PZ7.M879Mt 1991   91-2118
[E]—dc20   CIP
                           AC

Text © 1991 by Virginia Mueller.
Illustrations © 1991 by Lynn Munsinger.
Published in 1991 by Albert Whitman & Company,
6340 Oakton Street, Morton Grove, IL 60053-2723.
Published simultaneously in Canada by
General Publishing, Limited, Toronto.
All rights reserved. Printed in U.S.A.
10   9   8   7   6   5   4   3   2   1

For Abby Levine. V.M.

For Molly. L.M.

Monster's birthday party was fun until . . .

Monster got the hiccups.

Everyone tried to help.

Father turned Monster around and around,

but Monster said, "Hic! Hic!"

Sister and Baby scared Monster,

but Monster said, "Hic! Hic!"

Each friend gave Monster a hiccup hug,

but Monster still said, "Hic! Hic!"

Nothing helped,

not even standing on his head.

"Hic! Hic! HIC!" said Monster.

Then Mother brought in the cake.
The candles gave Monster an idea.
"I'll make a wish," Monster said.
"If I blow out all the candles,
my wish will come true."

Monster made a wish.
Then he took a BIG breath.
Everyone counted: 1, 2, 3 . . .

WHOOOSH!

Now Monster's birthday party was fun again.

His wish came true—
Monster's hiccups were gone!

ML   7/02